ANDROCLES AND THE LION

RETOLD AND ILLUSTRATED BY

Dennis Nolan

HARCOURT BRACE & COMPANY

SAN DIEGO   NEW YORK   LONDON

Requests for permission to make copies of any part of the
work should be mailed to:
Permissions Department, Harcourt Brace & Company,
6277 Sea Harbor Drive, Orlando,
Florida 32887-6777.

Library of Congress Cataloging-in-Publication Data
Nolan, Dennis.
Androcles and the lion/Dennis Nolan.
p.   cm.
Summary: A retelling of the fable in which
Androcles, a runaway slave, befriends a wounded lion.
ISBN 0-15-203355-6
[1. Fables.]   I. Title.
PZ8.2.N85An 1997 398.2
[E]—DC20 95-47578
First edition
A C E F D B
Printed in Singapore

Thank you, German.

For Bill, Marli, and Growl

Long ago, on the edge of the Egyptian desert, in the empire of Rome, a slave named Androcles was kept by a cruel master.

Each day Androcles rose to the sound of his master's voice: "Bring the jug of water, slave. Fetch my sandals. Fix my breakfast. Make my horses and chariot ready. More water, slave. And hurry."

Androcles did whatever his master ordered from sunrise to sunset, but even so, every day he felt the master's whip upon his back.

Androcles decided he must try to escape, though he knew he faced certain death if he were caught.

"I will run far into the desert," thought Androcles, "where no one can find me."

And so, one moonless night Androcles slipped away from his master's house and crept silently through the alleys of the city. Soon he passed the last building and walked out onto the warm, dark Egyptian sands. Before the first light of morning came, Androcles was away, deep into the desert.

For two days Androcles walked across the great desert. All he had to eat was the food he had taken from his master's house. On the third day his food was gone.

"I will be hungry," he thought. "But I would rather die of hunger than live one more day in my master's house."

The endless dunes rolled away in front of him. Swirling winds blew sand into his eyes. Not a single cloud covered the blazing sun.

"I would rather feel the burn of the sun on my back than the sting of my master's whip," Androcles said to himself.

Thirsty and exhausted, he came at last to a rocky hillside, where, deep in the shadows, he saw the mouth of a large, dark cave.

Cautiously Androcles stepped inside. The cool rock floor soothed his burning feet. Finding a spring of fresh water, he drank his fill, and when he felt sure he was alone, he walked to the back of the cave.

"A perfect place to hide," he thought. "No one will find me here."

But suddenly a great shadow blocked the doorway. Androcles froze in terror as an enormous lion entered and moved silently toward him.

Androcles stared into the fiery eyes of the great beast and heard its heavy breathing as it came closer. The lion bared its sharp white teeth and Androcles began to weep.

"Oh," he lamented, "to have finally escaped my cruel master only to be eaten by a lion."

He crouched, trembling, in the corner of the cave, waiting for the lion to roar and pounce upon him. But the lion did not roar. It only moaned and crept slowly forward, holding out its paw as if to ask for help.

"Oh, you're hurt," said Androcles.

A huge thorn was embedded in the soft flesh of the lion's paw. The lion groaned in pain, and Androcles forgot his fear. He gently patted the lion's shaggy mane and reached for its paw.

"Don't worry," he said. "I can pull that out for you."

He gripped the thorn firmly, and with a quick pull wrenched it free.

The lion lay down on the rocks purring like a kitten, and Androcles laughed. The lion licked its wound clean and then licked Androcles' face in gratitude. Soon, curled together in the cool darkness of the cave, Androcles and the lion were fast asleep.

After that day Androcles and the lion were the best of friends. The lion brought food to Androcles, and Androcles brought companionship to the lion. By day they hunted and explored the desert near the rocky hillside, and by night they slept safely in their cave.

"I am a free man," thought Androcles as he listened to the gentle snoring of the sleeping lion. "A happy man."

It was hard to remember what life had been like before he had come to the desert and met the lion.

For three years Androcles and the lion lived peacefully together. But one day, as Androcles was dozing in the shadows of the cliffs, Roman soldiers came upon him.

"A runaway slave!" they shouted as they jumped on Androcles and bound him tightly.

While they carried him away Androcles looked for the lion but saw only the empty desert.

The soldiers returned Androcles to his master's house only to be ordered away.

"I have no further need of him," said his angry master. "Take him to Rome and throw him to the beasts."

In the city of Rome stood a grand arena called the Circus Maximus. Sometimes slaves were taken there for punishment. Behind the walls ferocious animals were kept in cages. Crowds of people came to watch as the wild beasts were let loose to attack the helpless slaves.

On certain days the emperor Tiberius would visit the arena, and dine on rich food and drink while he watched the battles in the dirt below. It was on one of these days that Androcles arrived at the Circus Maximus.

Androcles squinted at the light as a soldier led him into the arena. Hundreds upon hundreds of people roared with anticipation. Androcles could hear the snarling and snapping of the hungry animals waiting to be let loose.

"Halt," ordered the soldier when Androcles had reached the center of the arena.

Androcles looked toward the emperor, who was eating figs and drinking from a large golden goblet. Slowly Tiberius raised his hand, and a hush fell upon the crowd. Androcles waited, alone and afraid, unarmed, under the boiling sun.

"Let it begin," commanded the emperor.

The soldiers raised a heavy metal gate.

An enormous lion moved out into the sun. It shook its great mane and pawed angrily at the ground when it saw Androcles. The people roared and stomped their feet in excitement. Androcles fell to his knees and waited helplessly for the lion to attack. It growled a warning and raced toward him.

But suddenly the lion stopped and Androcles looked right into its glowing eyes.

The two old friends recognized each other and the lion pranced playfully forward. "It's you," Androcles cried. "So they caught you, too." The lion licked Androcles' face and hands, and Androcles laughed aloud.

The astounded crowd broke into mighty cheers as Androcles and the lion rolled playfully in the dirt. Once again the emperor raised his hand. The crowd grew quiet.

"Have that man brought before me," Tiberius ordered.

Androcles walked across the arena with the faithful lion at his side. The emperor glared down at them.

"Tell us, slave, why this lion has spared your life."

Androcles told the story of his escape to the desert and his meeting with the lion and how they had become friends. The emperor listened quietly, then rose from his seat.

"We shall let the people decide your fate," he said, "whether you shall be put to death or set free." He ordered that Androcles' story be written on tablets and carried about the circus.

In the silence Androcles hung his head and waited. He stroked the lion's mane, wondering what would become of them. Then the crowd began to chant, "Free them! Free them!"

The people had decided. Androcles and the lion were led out of the arena.

Androcles marched in triumph through the streets with the lion beside him. As they passed shops and houses the people showered them with coins and threw flowers on the lion's golden mane. And everyone who saw them said, "This is the lion that was a man's best friend, and this is the man who healed the lion."

Androcles and the lion were free at last.

AUTHOR'S NOTE

The original story of Androcles and the Lion was written about A.D. 40 by Apion, an Egyptian who lived in Rome during the reign of the emperor Tiberius. Apion witnessed an incident at the Circus Maximus in which a lion really did spare the life of a slave. This was the basis of the story Apion wrote as "Androcles and the Lion" and included in his book *Ægyptiaca*. Though this book has not survived, during the second century A.D. the Roman Aulus Gellius copied selections from it for his *Noctes Atticae*, a twenty-book collection of writings on history, philosophy, biography, and other topics. Thirteen hundred years later, in A.D. 1469, this collection, which included Apion's tale as well as works by Aesop, Plutarch, and others, was finally gathered together and published in one volume. The story of Androcles and the Lion has since been translated and retold many, many times. A translation of Aulus Gellius' transcription of Apion's original was used as the basis of this retelling.